D0997924

ROALD DAHL's

BEASTLY CREATURES

 working in partnership with National Literacy Trust

ILLUSTRATED BY QUENTIN BLAKE

PUFFIN

PUFFIN BOOKS

UK | USA | Canada | Ireland | Australia
India | New Zealand | South Africa

Puffin Books is part of the Penguin Random House group of companies
whose addresses can be found at global.penguinrandomhouse.com.

puffinbooks.com

Penguin
Random House
UK

Made for McDonald's 2015

001

The Enormous Crocodile: first published in Great Britain by Jonathan Cape 1978
The Witches: first published in Great Britain by Jonathan Cape 1990
Published in paperback by Puffin Books

Printed in Slovakia

A CIP catalogue record for this book is available from the British Library

ISBN: 978–0–141–36250–2

The National Literacy Trust is a registered charity no. 1116260 and a company limited
by guarantee no. 5836486 registered in England and Wales and a registered charity in
Scotland no. SC042944. Registered address: 68 South Lambeth Road, London SW8 1RL.
National Literacy Trust logo and reading tips copyright © National Literacy Trust, 2014

www.literacytrust.org.uk/donate

Batch nr.: 123974/16

FSC
MIX
FSC® C022120

Explore the extraordinary world of

ROALD DAHL

But watch out!
BEASTLY CREATURES lurk within it.

Meet the **ENORMOUS CROCODILE**.
He thinks he is the bravest croc in the whole river.
He's full of **Clever Tricks** in his search for **juicy,
yummy** children . . . **for lunch!**

And do you know which beastly creatures
have **claws** like a cat, are **bald** as boiled eggs
and can smell **stink-waves** oozing out
of children? Why, **The Witches** of course!

For even more fun, don't miss the amazing
Happy Studio app. Download it now
to a phone or tablet and you'll get
fantastic extra activities for this book.

Clever Tricks

from

THE ENORMOUS CROCODILE

'Now for a very Clever Trick!' the Enormous Crocodile said to himself. 'This one is certain to work!'

There were no children in the playground at that moment. They were all in school.

The Enormous Crocodile found a large piece of wood and placed it in the middle of the playground. Then he lay across the piece of wood and tucked in his feet so that he looked almost exactly like a see-saw.

When school was over, the children

all came running on to the playground.

'Oh look!' they cried. 'We've got a new see-saw.'

They all crowded round, shouting with excitement.

'Bags I have the first go!'

'I'll get on the other end!'

'I want to go first!'

'So do I! So do I!'

Then, a girl who was older than the others said, 'It's rather a funny knobbly sort of a see-saw, isn't it? Do you think it'll be safe to sit on?'

'Of course it will!' the others said. 'It looks strong as anything!'

The Enormous Crocodile opened one eye just a tiny bit and watched the children who were crowding around him. 'Soon,' he thought, 'one of them is going to sit on my head, then I will give a jerk and a snap, and after that it will be *yum yum yum.*'

At that moment, there was a flash of brown and something jumped into the playground and hopped up on to the top of the swings.

It was Muggle-Wump, the Monkey.
'Run!' Muggle-Wump shouted to
the children. 'All of you, run, run,
run! That's not a see-saw! It's the
Enormous Crocodile
and he wants to eat
you up!'
The children
screamed and

ran for their lives.

Muggle-Wump disappeared back into the jungle, and the Enormous Crocodile was left all alone in the playground.

He cursed the Monkey and waddled back into the bushes to hide.

'I'm getting hungrier and hungrier!'
he said. 'I shall have to eat at least four
children now before I am full up!'

The Enormous Crocodile crept
around the edge of the town, taking
great care not to be seen.

He came to a place where they were getting ready to have a fair. There were slides and swings and dodgem-cars and people selling popcorn and candy-floss. There was also a big roundabout.

The roundabout had marvellous wooden creatures for the children to ride on. There were white horses and lions and tigers and mermaids with fishes' tails and fearsome dragons with red tongues sticking out of their mouths.

'Now for my next Clever Trick,' said the Enormous Crocodile, licking his lips.

When no one was looking, he crept up on to the roundabout and put himself between a wooden lion and a fearsome dragon. He sat up a bit on his back legs and he kept very still. He looked exactly like a wooden crocodile on the roundabout.

Soon, all sorts of children came flocking into the fair. Several of them ran towards the roundabout.

14

They were very excited.

'I'm going to ride on a dragon!' cried one.

'I'm going on a lovely white horse!' cried another.

'I'm going on a lion!' cried a third one.

And one little girl whose name was Jill said, 'I'm going to ride on that funny old wooden crocodile!'

The Enormous Crocodile kept very still, but he could see the little girl coming towards him. 'Yummy-yum-

yum,' he thought. 'I'll gulp her up easily in one gollop.'

Suddenly there was a *swish* and a *swoosh* and something came swishing and swooshing out of the sky.

It was the Roly-Poly Bird.

He flew round and round the roundabout, singing, 'Look out, Jill! Look out! Look out! Don't ride on that crocodile!'

Jill stopped and looked up.

'That's not a wooden crocodile!' sang the Roly-Poly Bird. 'It's a real one! It's the Enormous Crocodile from the river and he wants to eat you up!'

Jill turned and ran. So did all the other children. Even the man who was working the roundabout jumped off it

and ran away as fast as he could.

The Enormous Crocodile cursed the Roly-Poly Bird and waddled back into the bushes to hide.

'I'm so hungry now,' he said to himself, 'I could eat six children before I am full up!'

Just outside the town, there was a pretty little field with trees and bushes all round it. This was called The Picnic Place. There were several wooden tables and long benches, and people were allowed to go there and have a

picnic at any time. The Enormous
Crocodile crept over to The Picnic
Place. There was no one in sight.

'Now for another Clever Trick!' he
whispered to himself.

He picked a lovely bunch of flowers
and arranged it on one of the tables.

From the same table, he took away one of the benches and hid it in the bushes.

Then he put himself in the place where the bench had been.

By tucking his head under his chest, and by twisting his tail out of sight, he made himself look very much like a long wooden bench with four legs.

Soon, two boys and two girls came along carrying baskets of food. They were all from one family, and their mother had said they could go out and have a picnic together.

'Which table shall we sit at?' said one.

'Let's take the table with the lovely flowers on it,' said another.

The Enormous Crocodile kept as quiet as a mouse. 'I shall eat them all,' he said to himself. 'They will come and sit on my back and I will swizzle my head around quickly, and after that it'll be *squish crunch gollop*.'

Suddenly a big deep voice from the jungle shouted, 'Stand back, children! Stand back! Stand back!'

The children stopped and stared at the
place where the voice was coming from.

Then, with a crashing of branches,
Trunky the Elephant came rushing out
of the jungle.

'That's not a bench you were going to sit on!' he bellowed. 'It's the Enormous Crocodile, and he wants to eat you all up!'

Trunky trotted over to the spot where the Enormous Crocodile was standing, and quick as a flash he wrapped his trunk around the Crocodile's tail and hoisted him up into the air.

'Hey! Let me go!' yelled the Enormous Crocodile, who was now dangling upside down. 'Let me go! Let me go!'

'No,' Trunky said. 'I will not let you go. We've all had quite enough of your clever tricks.'

The ENORMOUS CROCODILE
wants to find his favourite feast.
If you were a BEASTLY CREATURE what
would you make into an **extraordinary** meal?
Describe it below then draw a picture of it.

....

....

....

....

....

I want to fill my
EMPTY TUMMY
with something **yummy
yummy YUMMY!**

Do you have the **Happy Studio** app downloaded? Launch it **now** for an **extra** activity!

How to Recognize a Witch

from

THE WITCHES

The next evening, after my grandmother had given me my bath, she took me once again into the living-room for another story.

'Tonight,' the old woman said, 'I am going to tell you how to recognize a witch when you see one.'

'Can you always be sure?' I asked.

'No,' she said, 'you can't. And that's the trouble. But you can make a pretty good guess.'

'In the first place,' she said, 'a REAL WITCH is certain always to be wearing

gloves when you meet her.'

'Surely not *always*,' I said. 'What about in the summer when it's hot?'

'Even in the summer,' my grandmother said. 'She has to. Do you want to know why?'

'Why?' I said.

'Because she doesn't have finger-nails. Instead of finger-nails, she has thin curvy claws, like a cat, and she wears the gloves to hide them. Mind you, lots of very respectable women wear gloves, especially in winter, so this doesn't help you very much.'

'Mamma used to wear gloves,' I said.

'Not in the house,' my grandmother

said. 'Witches wear gloves even in the house. They only take them off when they go to bed.'

'How do you know all this, Grandmamma?'

'Don't interrupt,' she said. 'Just take it all in. The second thing to remember is that a REAL WITCH is always bald.'

'*Bald?*' I said.

'Bald as a boiled egg,' my grandmother said.

I was shocked. There was something indecent about a bald woman. 'Why are they bald, Grandmamma?'

'Don't ask me why,' she snapped. 'But you can take it from me that not a single hair grows on a witch's head.'

'How horrid!'

'Disgusting,' my grandmother said.

'If she's bald, she'll be easy to spot,' I said.

'Not at all,' my grandmother said. 'A REAL WITCH always wears a wig to hide her baldness. She wears a first-class wig. And it is almost impossible to tell a really first-class wig from ordinary hair unless you give it a pull to see if it comes off.'

'Then that's what I'll have to do,' I said.

'Don't be foolish,' my grandmother said. 'You can't go round pulling at the hair of every lady you meet, even if shc is wearing gloves. Just you try it and see what happens.'

'So that doesn't help much either,' I said.

'None of these things is any good on its own,' my grandmother said. 'It's only when you put them all together that they begin to make a little sense. Mind you,' my grandmother went on,

'these wigs do cause a rather serious problem for witches.'

'What problem, Grandmamma?'

'They make the scalp itch most terribly,' she said. 'You see, when an actress wears a wig, or if you or I were

to wear a wig, we would be putting it on over our own hair, but a witch has to put it straight on to her naked scalp. And the underneath of a wig is always very rough and scratchy. It sets up a frightful itch on the bald skin. It causes nasty sores on the head. Wig-rash, the witches call it. And it doesn't half itch.'

'What other things must I look for to recognize a witch?' I asked.

'Look for the nose-holes,' my grandmother said. 'Witches have slightly larger nose-holes than ordinary people. The rim of each nose-hole is pink and curvy, like the rim of a certain kind of sea-shell.'

'Why do they have such big nose-holes?' I asked.

'For smelling with,' my grandmother said. 'A REAL WITCH has the most amazing powers of smell. She can actually smell out a child who is standing on the other side of the street on a pitch-black night.'

'She couldn't smell me,' I said. 'I've just had a bath.'

'Oh yes she could,' my grandmother

said. 'The cleaner you happen to be, the more smelly you are to a witch.'

'That can't be true,' I said.

'An absolutely clean child gives off the most ghastly stench to a witch,' my grandmother said. 'The dirtier you are, the less you smell.'

'But that doesn't make sense, Grandmamma.'

'Oh yes it does,' my grandmother said. 'It isn't the *dirt* that the witch is smelling. It is *you*. The smell that drives a witch mad actually comes right out of your own skin. It comes oozing out of your skin in waves, and these waves, stink-waves the witches call them, go floating through the air and hit the witch right smack in her nostrils. They send her reeling.'

'Now wait a minute, Grandmamma . . .'

'Don't interrupt,' she said. 'The point is this. When you haven't washed for a week and your skin is all covered over with dirt, then quite obviously the stink-waves cannot come oozing out nearly so strongly.'

'I shall never have a bath again,' I said.

'Just don't have one too often,' my

grandmother said. 'Once a month is quite enough for a sensible child.'

It was at moments like these that I loved my grandmother more than ever.

'Grandmamma,' I said, 'if it's a dark night, how can a witch smell the difference between a child and a grown-up?'

'Because grown-ups don't give out stink-waves,' she said. 'Only children do that.'

'But I don't *really* give out stink-waves, do I?' I said. 'I'm not giving them out at this very moment, am I?'

'Not to me you aren't,' my grandmother said. 'To me you are smelling like raspberries and cream.

But to a witch you would be smelling
absolutely disgusting.'

 'What would I be smelling of?' I asked.

 'Dogs' droppings,' my grandmother
said.

I reeled. I was stunned. '*Dogs'*
droppings!' I cried. 'I am *not* smelling of
dogs' droppings! I don't believe it!
I *won't* believe it!'

'What's more,' my grandmother
said, speaking with a touch of relish,
'to a witch you'd be smelling of *fresh*
dogs' droppings.'

'That simply is not true!' I cried.
'I know I am not smelling
of dogs' droppings,
stale or fresh!'

'There's no point in arguing about it,' my grandmother said. 'It's a fact of life.'

I was outraged. I simply couldn't bring myself to believe what my grandmother was telling me.

'So if you see a woman holding her nose as she passes you in the street,' she went on, 'that woman could easily be a witch.'

I decided to change the subject. 'Tell me what else to look for in a witch,' I said.

'The eyes,' my grandmother said. 'Look carefully at the eyes, because the eyes of a REAL WITCH are different from yours and mine. Look in the middle of each eye where there is normally a little black dot. If she is a witch, the black dot will keep changing colour, and you will see fire and you will see ice dancing right in the very centre of the coloured dot. It will send shivers running all over your skin.'

My grandmother leaned back in her chair. I squatted on the floor, staring

up at her, fascinated. She was not
smiling. She looked deadly serious.

'What else is different about them,
Grandmamma?'

'The feet,' she said. 'Witches never have toes.'

'No toes!' I cried. 'Then what do they have?'

'They just have feet,' my grandmother said. 'The feet have square ends with no toes on them at all.'

'Does that make it difficult to walk?' I asked.

'Not at all,' my grandmother said. 'But it does give them a problem with their shoes. All ladies like to wear small rather pointed shoes, but a witch, whose feet are very wide and square at the ends, has the most awful job squeezing her feet into those neat little pointed shoes.'

'Why doesn't she wear wide comfy shoes with square ends?' I asked.

'She dare not,' my grandmother

said. 'Just as she hides her baldness with a wig, she must also hide her ugly witch's feet by squeezing them into pretty shoes.'

'Isn't that terribly uncomfortable?' I said.

'Extremely uncomfortable,' my grandmother said. 'But she has to put up with it.'

'If she's wearing ordinary shoes, it won't help me to recognize her, will it, Grandmamma?'

'I'm afraid it won't,' my grandmother

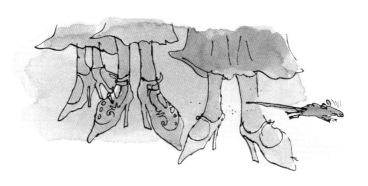

said. 'You might possibly see her
limping very slightly, but only if you
were watching closely.'

'Are those the only differences then,
Grandmamma?'

'There's one more,' my grandmother
said. 'Just one more.'

'What is it, Grandmamma?'

'Their spit is blue.'

'Blue!' I cried. 'Not blue! Their spit can't be *blue*!'

'Blue as a bilberry,' she said.

'You don't mean it, Grandmamma! Nobody can have blue spit!'

'Witches can,' she said.

'Is it like ink?' I asked.

'Exactly,' she said. 'They even use it to write with. They use those old-fashioned pens that have nibs and they simply lick the nib.'

'Can you *notice* the blue spit,
Grandmamma? If a witch was talking
to me, would I be able to notice it?'

'Only if you looked carefully,' my
grandmother said. 'If you looked very

carefully you would probably see a slight bluish tinge on her teeth. But it doesn't show much.'

'It would if she spat,' I said.

'Witches never spit,' my grandmother said. 'They daren't.'

Then she added, 'So there you are. That's about all I can tell you. None of it is very helpful. You can still never be absolutely sure whether a woman is a witch or not just by looking at her. But if she is wearing the gloves, if she has the large nose-holes, the queer eyes and the hair that looks as though it might be a wig, and if she has a bluish tinge on her teeth – if she has all of these things, then you run like mad.'

Look carefully at these smiling ladies.
Can you tell they are really **WITCHES**?

Reveal the extraordinary truth by drawing a
picture of them with **curvy claws, bald heads**
and **large nose-holes**.

Don't forget **fiery eyes** and
a **blue tinge** to the teeth!

What **BEASTLY CREATURES**
you've created!

Do you have the
Happy Studio app
downloaded?
Launch it **now** for
an **extra** activity!

The BEASTLY CREATURES are everywhere!

The **Happy Studio** app has extra
activities linked to this book.
Download it now to
your phone or tablet.

And you can delve deeper into
the extraordinary world of

ROALD DAHL

at www.roalddahl.com